WITHDRAW

YA Jones
Jones, Patrick
Barrier

$7.95
ocn892982952
10/15/2014

BARRIER

THE ALTERNATIVE

BARRIER

PATRICK JONES

darby creek
MINNEAPOLIS

Text copyright © 2014 by Patrick Jones

All rights reserved. International copyright secured. No part of this book may be reproduced, stored in a retrieval system, or transmitted in any form or by any means—electronic, mechanical, photocopying, recording, or otherwise—without the prior written permission of Lerner Publishing Group, Inc., except for the inclusion of brief quotations in an acknowledged review.

Darby Creek
A division of Lerner Publishing Group, Inc.
241 First Avenue North
Minneapolis, MN 55401 USA

For updated reading levels and more information, look up this title at www.lernerbooks.com.

Cover and interior photographs © Zsolt Farkas/Dreamstime.com (girl); © iStockphoto.com/joeygil (locker background).

Main body text set in Janson Text LT Std 12/17.
Typeface provided by Linotype AG.

Library of Congress Cataloging-in-Publication Data

Jones, Patrick, 1961–
        Barrier / by Patrick Jones.
            pages   cm. — (The alternative)
        Summary: A new, alternative high school, psychotherapy, a romantic interest, and a manga club help tenth-grader Jessica cope with her social anxiety disorder.
        ISBN 978-1-4677-3899-6 (lib. bdg. : alk. paper)
        ISBN 978 1 4677 4632-8 (eBook)
        [1. Social phobia—Fiction. 2. Interpersonal relations—Fiction. 3. High schools—Fiction. 4. Schools—Fiction. 5. Psychotherapy—Fiction. 6. Family problems—Fiction. 7. Racially-mixed people—Fiction.] I. Title.
PZ7.J7242Bar 2014
[Fic]—dc23   2013041389

Manufactured in the United States of America
1 – BP – 7/15/14

WITH THANKS TO ANALEYSHA,
KIARA, AND NAYALIE
-P.J.

1

JESSICA IS SHY

"Jessica is just shy, that's all," Mom told the school counselor. It was what she'd told every counselor at every school, from my grade school in Stephenville, Texas, to tenth grade here at Harding High School in St. Paul. I wondered if the counselor noticed my mom nervously tapping her heel against the floor—what she did when she couldn't smoke away the stress. Mom hated closed-door dialogues as much as I did.

"Mrs. Johnson, I think it's more than that,"

Mrs. Something-or-Other retorted.

"I remember my first few days at a new school," Mom started, and she was off. The endless drama of Mary Johnson, the world's blandest name for the highest-strung creature on earth.

When Mom paused to take a breath, the school counselor jumped in. "On her first day, she skipped one class entirely and walked out of another in the middle of the period. Her second day was about the same, while yesterday was—" All eyes fell on my sweat-drenched, beet-red face.

Yesterday was a disaster of epic failures, I finished silently. *AKA a normal day in the life of Jessica Johnson, freak of nature. Half white, half black, and altogether crazy as a Minnesota loon.*

"I asked Jessica to do an online assessment," the counselor told Mom. I'd done the thing just to shut her up and get her to leave me alone, but now this. "This isn't official, but she tested very high, and given—"

"That's my girl—smart as her mom!" I glanced down at my manga.

"Mrs. Johnson, it was an assessment for social anxiety disorder. A high score indicates that she likely struggles with it." And then the school counselor was off and running. "People with social anxiety disorder generally experience extreme fear in social situations, which causes serious stress and impaired ability to function in daily life. Their fears can be triggered by perceived judgment, or real scrutiny, from others."

Hello, I want to shout, *I'm sitting right here as you call me crazy. Which I am, thank you.*

Mom pursed her thin lips while the toe tapping kicked into overdrive.

"I have some recommendations that I think might help your daughter succeed."

If you could smoke in school, Mom would have finished her third by now. Me, only one.

"First, Jessica should see a licensed therapist specializing in social anxiety disorder. I've recommended other students to Nina Martin, who has helped them get their lives back on track."

Mom nodded. Sure, therapy for me, but not for her. She's just fine . . . Please.

"Second, there are online support groups for

most illnesses and disorders. You should look into an online support community for social anxiety. She shouldn't do this until after she's made real progress in therapy, though."

I could ask Dad, I figured. He might even answer me for once. He's online almost twenty-four seven.

"Finally, I think maybe Harding might not be the best environment for Jessica. Rondo Alternative High School might be a better fit. It is much smaller—less than a hundred students. So the class sizes are small, and there's a real sense of community that might be hard for a student like Jessica to find at Harding without participating in after-school activities."

Mom should've been used to me needing to switch schools, but that caught her off-guard. After she'd recovered, she started to ask questions. All practical stuff: location (not that far away), cost (none), and other students (collection of head cases like me, it seemed).

"The downside of Rondo is that, while they have excellent staff and teachers, its small size means it has no library, no gym, few clubs, and no dedicated school counselors, so—"

"I want to go!" I shouted. *You had me at "no school counselors."* Plus, it sounded great to go where nobody knew I was crazy.

"Are you sure?" Mom asked in that you're-wrong tone that she does *so* right. I nodded my nappy head at the idea of another fresh start. Another chance to succeed; another chance to fail.

2

Where to Sit? What to Eat?

"Welcome to tenth-grade language arts," Mrs. Howard-Hernandez said to me with a big smile. I wanted to disappear. I also wished I was as pretty as she was, or could stand up in front of people and talk, or had a boyfriend, or had anything other than the fire-breathing dragon in my stomach as lunch approached. Not hunger—fear. Where to sit? What to eat? Could I even eat in front of others?

"For our first assignment, we'll be reading—"

Loud groans from some kids interrupted her.

"We'll be reading a book called *I Can't Keep My Own Secrets: Six-Word Memoirs by Teens.* Even if you don't like to read, you should like this book." I glance over her shoulder at the stuffed bookcase. The Harding counselor had lied: there is a school library, and it's in this room.

"What do you mean, 'six-word memoirs'?" some kid hollered.

The teacher paused with dramatic flair. "Teacher, Mother, Wife, I, love, life." People giggled.

"That's my life in six words. Let's get the books." She looked out at where she'd put me, in back on the left, toward the exit door. She must have been warned. "Jessica?"

The dragon roared as eyes descended on me. My owl-like hearing seized every whisper and verdict: "Is she white? Black? What's with her hair? Who dressed her, a blind man?" At least, that's what I think I heard.

"Jessica, would you and—" Her eyes searched the room. "And Dylan distribute the books to the class?" Dylan, a lanky black dude, sprang up from his chair, but I stayed planted.

"Jessica, please?" she repeated, still friendly but a little firmer. Not helping was causing more attention than helping would've. Once again, I'd made the wrong decision. That was twenty times already that day, if anyone was counting. Wait. Someone was. Me.

With my hideous plain black T-shirt and jeans that were too big for my skinny butt, I navigated my way toward the front of the room. I felt my heart beat in double-time.

As I handed out the books, a couple guys made eyes at me, sizing me up. As if. A couple of girls said thank you, and that's what I needed. Somebody so polite that she wouldn't push me away. My method was to find a girl who seemed gracious and attach myself to her like a barnacle to the hull of a ship. I didn't make friends so much as I donned human shields.

My black T showed pit sweat; it was a stupid choice I'd spent two hours making. I sat back down in my chair, exhausted in less than five minutes. And lunch hadn't even started yet. I'd need a place to collapse, not eat.

"As you probably guessed, your assignment will be for each of you to write six-word memoirs about yourself." Mrs. Howard-Hernandez was still all smiles. If I looked like her and didn't have these braces, I might smile more. "Then you'll present the best one to the class."

More groans and remarks from others, but I couldn't get out a single noise as panic rose up in me.

"Do we have to speak in front of class?" asked one of the "thank you" girls. Her hair, her top, and her jeans with a hole in them all indicated "loud," but she'd asked the right question. My ship had come in.

"Yes, Tonisha, you do. I know it's not something most of you enjoy, but the ability to present information is a key twenty-first century skill. I used to coach debate, so I'm happy to help anyone who'd like pointers for speaking in public. The presentation will be part of your grade for the project."

"How much a part?" Tonisha asked, with tons of attitude jammed into just four words.

"You can't get an A without doing it. Probably at best a C."

"Messed up, seriously messed up."

"Alright, let's get started. Open up to page one, and let's have Dylan start reading. Dylan?"

Dylan spoke first, but soon it would be my turn. That wasn't happening. Soon I was out the door. The pretty blond teacher called my name, but I didn't look back. Getting a C would be just fine.

3

Everybody Else Got the How-To Manual

"Darryl, why are you parking here?" Mom asked in that you're-so-stupid tone.

"It's a good spot," Dad answered. It was a great spot, right in front of the grocery store.

"But look at the ice machine." Mom pointed to the large machine against the wall of the store, at least ten feet away from the car. "What if something happens and it falls on the car?"

Dad didn't say a word, per usual. He grunted once and moved the car, adding more time to our shopping task. A task that probably took a normal family a half hour, but we'd be there twice that time, easy. We were running late because Mom decided to do laundry after I got home from school, and we couldn't leave the house with a machine running. She was too afraid the dryer would short out and catch fire or the washing machine would flood.

Inside the store, I avoided people staring at me by never looking up. My eyes didn't linger over the rows of fresh vegetables, the bogo sales, or the new and improved items—none of which Mom will buy ("You know those vegetables all have bugs on them," and, "If they're giving it away there must be something wrong with it," and "I liked the original version better"). Instead my eyes stayed focused on my phone like every other teenager's.

Except for one thing: other people's phones have numbers for friends stored in them, and mine didn't. Their phones buzzed and dinged with incoming texts; mine did not. Their phones enlarged their world; mine narrowed it further.

Dad pushed the cart, fiddled with his phone, and waited impatiently as Mom struggled to decide which salad dressing to purchase. Per usual, she picked one, put it in the cart, and just as Dad was about to move on, she changed her mind, removed it, put in another one, and off we went.

"I'm going to get dog food," I said after only two aisles of torture. As I walked away, deep into an online game, I accidently knocked over a display of cans. The eyes of every man, woman, and child turned toward my family: a six-foot-two, three-hundred-pound black man; his five-foot-one, whiter-than-white wife; and me, their skinny, mute, mutant offspring.

"Don't worry about it," I heard a voice say over the techno music my headphones pumped into my ears. I turned around. It was a boy, an older teen, dressed in a crisp, clean store uniform. He smiled at me, and my face went from blushing to way beyond red.

"You go to Rondo?" He was super cute, with thick black hair and a thin growth of facial hair.

I nodded.

"Me too. I'm a junior. My name's Juan. You're new, right? What grade are you in?"

For a second, I forgot how to talk to people. It's like everybody but me got the manual titled *How to Be a Normal Social Person.* "I'm in tenth grade."

"Nice." A smile and that was it. He focused on picking up my mess, and I ran away like a mouse.

I found the dog food that Maurice, my eight-year-old pug/beagle mix, liked. But I didn't pick it up. I just stood there and wished someone—Juan, Tonisha, anyone else—would come over and we'd talk and laugh, just like normal people did.

Before I pulled up new music, I flipped through pictures of Maurice. Maurice was my grandpa's dog. When Grandpa died, the dog came to live with us, a result of the only fight I'd ever won against my mom. I'd resorted to the "I'll throw myself down the stairs" ploy for the first time. It hasn't worked since, but Maurice was worth it. Dogs don't care what anyone thinks of them. They're very Zen animals. I'd rather be a dog than human any day.

With my parents across the store and nothing to distract me, I began to catalog everything stupid thing I'd said and done at school. I hadn't spoken, so that helped. I figured I'd talk later that week, but not at school. Dad was taking me to my first therapist appointment. I felt sorry for the good doctor in advance. I didn't need a therapist; I needed a miracle—except that I believe in Zen dogs, not gods.

4

ONE STEP FORWARD, TWO STEPS BACK

"Thanks," I mumbled to Skylar, who sold cigarettes dirt cheap. I didn't ask where he got them. I was just happy I didn't have to steal more from Mom.

"Any time," he said. He stuffed my money in his pocket. "What's your name?"

I stood there, unable to answer the obvious.

"My pal Juan there thinks you're cute." Skylar pointed at Juan Fernandez, the guy from the grocery store. I focused on the pack of More Menthols that rested in my sweaty left hand.

"You don't talk much, do you?" Skylar asked, but he smiled when he said it. Skylar had a hard shell, probably toughened by hard times, but it seemed like deep down there was a sweet kid trying to escape.

"If you wanna hang with us, he'd like that." And then he was gone, headed back into school with his friends for lunch. They'd eat, laugh, and talk about weekend plans. I stood outside in the brisk fall air alone, away from even the other smokers. The second day of school, I'd tried to mix with them, but they were so loud, it just made my silence somehow stand out more.

If you're going to stand alone, then have a cigarette so you don't look like a loser. That was the best advice I ever got in my failed ninth-grade year at Verdant Hill. It was the wisdom of Tim Watts, my only friend and my crush until he broke my heart. Like every other school, Rondo was full of cliques, so once again, Tim's advice applied. As I inhaled, I thought, *Here's to you, Tim.*

○ ○ ○

"Tonisha Hyun," Mrs. Howard-Hernandez said, although I barely heard her words as my eyelids closed. I hadn't slept again last night.

Tonisha stayed in her seat and made the teacher call her again. What was going on?

"I'm reading it from my seat," Tonisha said. She narrowed her heavily made-up eyes.

Mrs. Howard-Hernandez frowned, a rare sight on her face. "The assignment was—"

"To write ten six-word memoirs and read one aloud to the class." Tonisha clutched the paper with the assignment in her left hand. "It didn't say nothin' bout standing up."

"Everyone else has—"

"I ain't everyone else," Tonisha said. "So here goes. Sweet not sour, manga not gangsta."

A couple of people applauded—maybe not so much for the memoir as for the attitude. I tried not to stare, still figuring her out. She hung with a group of smart black girls, but I'd also seen her talking with the Asian gangsta boys.

Tonisha passed her paper to the student in front of her. Eventually it made it to the front. Mrs. Howard-Hernandez reacted simply by writing a grade on it and calling the next name.

I covered my metal-and-rubber-band-filled mouth to stifle another yawn. I'd stood in front of the mirror until three in the morning practicing. It was only six words. I could do this.

She was going in alphabetical order, not by the seating chart. As a J, I was right in the middle.

Some of the memoirs were funny, and some were sad, but all were revealing. Mine, like me, said nothing.

"Rashad Jefferson," Mrs. Howard-Hernandez called out. Rashad walked to the front of the room, all six feet three inches of him, so confident like he owned the place. He read his memoir to lots of applause. It was almost my turn. My ears ached as the dragon roared from within.

"Leigh Jones." Another name, another six words.

"Jessica Johnson." I stood and took one step toward the front of room. I clutched the paper like it was a life raft, but it couldn't save me. One step forward, two steps back. Then out the door.

5

No Drama, No Trauma, Just No Friends

Therapist Nina Martin's office didn't reek of tears like I'd expected. There were lots of earth tones, a bookcase with paperbacks on top and toys on the bottom, and plenty of framed diplomas filling the wall of the small space. After an awkward greeting—I didn't know any other kind—she showed me a clipboard with a paper attached to it. "It's not a pop quiz," she said, and laughed.

There was something about her manner that

put me at ease, almost. She looked older than Mom, maybe in her forties, and she wore a sharp blue suit. The yellow flowers in the room complemented her blond hair. Perfect makeup too.

"Jessica, we're going to start with a diagnostic instrument that will give me the information I need to help us put together a treatment plan, if that's what's called for."

"What do you mean *if*?" I asked. She set the clipboard down and leaned closer to me.

"I believe you were referred by the school counselor at Harding, and she—"

"I don't go to Harding anymore."

"Really?" She wrote that down on the pad of paper now resting against her knee. "Why?"

I told her that story. I told her all about Rondo and my ninth-grade hell at Verdant Hill, spoiled rich-kid central out in the burbs.

"You don't seem to have any problem talking to me!" she joked.

I laughed, not too loud. "That's because you already know that I'm crazy, right?"

"You think you're crazy?" she asked calmly. She scribbled on the pad again. She started to speak but then stopped. It was like when Dad and I played chess. He'd be touching the pawn for minutes but then move the knight. "So, tell me a little bit about your family history."

I gave her that story too. "My dad was from here in St. Paul, but he played football on scholarship at a small college in Texas. My mom was from the college town, Stephenville. I don't actually know how they met. They never told me, and I guess I never asked. I do know that not long after they met, they ran away and got married, and then I came along seven months later. So, I guess they had to get married back then, especially in a small town like that."

"When did you move to St. Paul?" she asked.

"Well, Dad dropped out of college and got a job doing computer stuff," I said. "We moved here just before I started fifth grade, partly to be near my grandfather, who was sick."

"That must have been traumatic for you, moving away from your friends."

I paused. She had to bring up those memories of having friends. "I had lots of friends in Texas, and I didn't want to move, but it's not like

I got a say or anything."

"How about once you moved here? Did you make friends right away?"

Another pause. "Well, at first, but then . . ."

"But then?"

"In junior high, everything changed. I don't know why."

"The transition from elementary school can be very difficult for lots of children," she said, as if to reassure me that I was normal. As if. "Did you make new friends in junior high?"

The box of tissues was out of reach. Fine—I would just use my long sleeves. "Not really."

Like some mind reader, she handed me the tissues. "Do you know why?"

I wanted a great story to tell her. Some shower room ordeal like in the movie *Carrie*, or an embarrassing nipple-slip, but no. I had no drama, no trauma, just no friends. "No. I don't." The tears spilled over.

She let me cry for a while. Finally, she said, "Jessica, we need to do this test."

I sucked it up. I felt like I'd just taken one, except I didn't know if I had passed or failed.

EIGHTEEN QUESTIONS THAT DEFINE MY LIFE

"I'm going to present you with eighteen social situations," Nina Martin said. "I want you to tell me—on a scale of zero to three, with three being the highest—how much stress you feel in each situation. Also, on the same scale, how much you avoid each situation."

I nodded. I'd known this was coming. The second I'd gotten home from the Harding counselor's office, I started to look up stuff online about social anxiety disorder. She was using something called the Kutcher Generalized Social Anxiety Disorder Scale for Adolescents. I'd printed it out and studied it. There was one big question for me to consider over all eighteen items: did I want to answer honestly and maybe deal with all this, or should I just lie and avoid it?

"Even though we're running late, I want you to take your time answering," she explained, trying to sound so reassuring. "Some people need more time to process."

I laughed to myself as I thought about Mom agonizing over which salad dressing to buy, or Dad alone in the basement all the time on his computer, and me turning into them. They were isolated, paralyzed by indecision.

"Remember, scale of zero to three. Ready?" My firm nod was the go-ahead sign.

"One: initiating conversation with a member of the opposite sex. Zero to three?"

"That's a bad question," I said. "I mean, what if I was gay or bi? I'm not, but what if?"

"Excellent point, Jessica. Let's say, then, a member of the sex to which you are attracted."

Pause. A quick flash to Juan. "Is there a four?"

She scribbled on the paper. "Zero to three: how much you avoid that situation."

"Normally, boys avoid me," I joked, but her eyes stayed focus on the test. "Three."

"Next, attending a party or other social gathering with people you don't know very well."

"I'm sorry, but is there a 'does not apply' choice?" I said. "I haven't been to a party here."

"I guess, imagine if that would happen, what your stress level would be. Zero to three."

"Three." I had figured I'd give the avoidance items lots of twos and threes, when I'd looked over the test on my own. Except it was weird to think about whether I avoid social things. Usually it just seemed like a social life avoided me.

As we went through the rest of the test, I answered threes to most of the items on school situations. After what happened in language arts, there was no pretending how I felt about "presenting in front of a small group or in a classroom setting." What about participating in class discussions? Or joining a class or social group once the class or activity was already underway?

Most of the items about body image stuff—changing in a locker room, showering in a common shower—weren't a big deal for me. I guess because that part of me, save being biracial with nightmare hair, was pretty normal. I hate my body clothed, and I hate my body naked. I'm pretty average.

I gave twos for speaking with strangers and authority figures, but then I kicked back to "Why aren't there fives?" on items like eating in public, going to a party, and asking someone out. Adults didn't bother me; I guess there's a reason they call it *peer* pressure.

Nina Martin asked what my three biggest stressors were. I didn't even have to pause before I blurted them out: speaking in class, talking to a cute guy, and going to a party. The holy trinity of terror.

"Now, we'll finish with the distress quotient," she said way too calmly. "Same idea. Zero to three on how strongly you react to each of these items in most social situations. Ready? Item one: feeling embarrassed or humiliated."

"Three," I said, "and I'll save us some time. Three to the first eight items, down to 'sweating.' Give me a big three on all of them."

She eyed me carefully. "So you know the test?" she asked with an edge in her tone. "Okay, then the final three items?"

"Zero. I don't feel the need to run to use bathroom, and I don't shake or tremble," I said. *But*, I thought, *your stupid scale doesn't ask about the reaction I know best: crying uncontrollably.*

7

BLACK WHITE BROWN, NEW IN TOWN

I stared down at the piece of paper in front of me. My first six-word memoir had earned the first F of my school career.

"Jessica, do you know why I failed you?" Mrs. Howard-Hernandez asked. I gave a small head shake. I sat with her, Mrs. Baker, the school principal, and Mr. Aaron, an educational assistant, around a small table in a conference room. This was my first "check-in," which I'd overheard other students talking about. It seemed more like three hanging judges and one defendant.

"Your scores from junior high, last year at Verdant Hill, and on your placement tests were excellent," Mrs. Baker said. "And on much of your work so far here at Rondo, you've excelled."

"But you didn't fulfill the terms of the assignment," Mrs. Howard-Hernandez said.

"Did you fail Tonisha too?" I asked in a little-bird voice.

"I can't tell you what grade I gave another student," she countered. "This isn't about Tonisha. All you needed to do was to stand up and say six words in front of the class."

Mrs. Howard-Hernandez pointed at the paper in my hand. It was my assignment: ten six-word memoirs. My name was in black type at top of the page, along with a big red hand-written F. "Which of these would you have read in front of the class? Which is the best one? Which best describes you?"

I pointed at the last one.

"Can you read it to us?"

I took a breath. "Black, white, brown, new in

town." Mr. Aaron applauded.

"Jessica, that's very good," Mrs. Baker said. "So from now on, can we count on you to participate more?" Like it was that simple.

"I don't like to talk in class. What's the big deal?" I fought back.

"Rondo isn't just another school; we're a community of learners," Mrs. Baker said. "We believe students learn best not just from teachers, but from other students."

I hid my mouth. All my classes had way too much group work, which to me was any group work. Most of the time I got in groups with Tonisha. She took over the discussion, which was fine by me.

"Maybe you're not challenged enough," Mrs. Baker continued. "Many students come to Rondo because they're behind in earning credits, but you skipped a grade in elementary school."

Was that the start of it? Was skipping fourth grade when we moved the beginning of my fall?

"Since your scores in math and science have always been excellent, we've decided—if you and your parents agree—to jump you ahead to eleventh grade in both math and science."

More strangers and cliques, my head screamed, but Juan was in eleventh grade. "Okay."

"In your other classes, we'll keep you in tenth," Mrs. Baker continued. "This will also expose you to more students here at Rondo, which might help you in other ways."

I didn't need to ask what that meant. It meant they'd noticed I was a loner oddball.

"What about this F?" I asked Mrs. Howard-Hernandez. She motioned for the paper.

"I'll change this to an incomplete," she said. "You need to finish the assignment."

I handed the paper back to her. She crossed out the F and returned it to me. "Look, Jessica, I taught debate at my last high school, so I know that many students don't like to—"

"I don't want to do it," I said, fighting back tears. "But I won't fail anything."

No one laughed at the irony—that I failed at just about everything except most schoolwork.

"Here's one other thing to consider," Mr. Aaron said in his normal upbeat tone. I wasn't fooled. "I've noticed in SSR that a number of students, including you, read Japanese comics."

"Manga."

"I'm putting together a lunchtime manga club," he said. "Would you like to join it?"

§

IF ONLY LIFE COULD BE EASY

After dinner, the set-in-stone Johnson routine
began. Mom cleared the table a dish at a time,
turning a five-minute task into an hour-long
project. She'd slowly wash each dish, glass, and
piece of silverware by hand, not trusting the
dishwasher Dad had bought a few years ago.
("What if it floods the house? What if it misses
a spot?") At the same time, she coated each dish
with a thin layer of smoke, sometimes going
through half a pack in an hour. By the time she

finished the first smoke or dish, Dad would be downstairs on the computer, doing whatever it is he always did. I'd given up asking.

"I'm taking Maurice for a walk," I said into the void. The word *walk* triggered Maurice's animal excitement, just like *group* triggered my human flight response.

As I put the leash on my best friend, I glanced at the three family photos over the mantel of the fireplace (sealed off to ease Mom's fear of a spontaneous fire starting, of course). The first picture was my parents' wedding photo: Mom looked excited, while Dad looked maybe slightly happier than his usual look of indifference. The second starred me as a baby in Dad's arms, Mom by his side, with their expressions reversed from the first photo—except she didn't look indifferent so much as scared. Finally, the photo of my first day at school, where we're all on the same page: worried. Those were the only photos up in the house, like nothing else ever happened to us.

I waited to light up until I got to the park about a half mile from our house. My parents probably knew, but Mom lacked moral authority on this issue, and Dad lacked, well, everything. He wasn't a bad parent, he just wasn't much of one. He provided, and for him, that seemed enough.

Once in the park, I made a beeline for the swings. With the long pink leash in my right hand and a cigarette in my left, I swung back and forth, feeling lighter than air. If only life could be this easy. But life was hard, and I made it harder. As I leaped off the swing, I knew what I needed: a time machine.

After I finished the smoke, I pulled out my phone. Mrs. Baker was right about my math skills, in part because I had a good memory. Could I recall the number I'd erased in a crying fit?

"Tim, it's Jessica Johnson," I said, probably sounding startled that he picked up.

In the long pause that followed, my stomach turned over and over.

"Sorry, I shouldn't have called," I said, and I started to hang up. I shouldn't have dialed his number.

"Jessica, hey! Sorry, I was in the middle of eating," he finally replied. "How are you?"

A thousand thoughts raced through my mind. Usually, when I knew I'd have to talk with someone, I'd make notes and think out every possible question and answer, except with Tim.

"Okay," I lied, because the truth was a mess. "How is Verdant Hill?"

Tim, as always, took over the conversation. Verdant Hill was this expensive and well-regarded private school, but it was full of bullies and backstabbing cliques. There he'd excelled, as I had failed, in all things from band to theater to making friends. Why did he need more friends? He had me. As a friend, although I wished it could've been more. "*Jessica, wow, but I think we should just be friends,*" he'd said.

"You doing any better with . . ." he started. In my Verdant Hill days, we didn't know I had social anxiety disorder. I thought I was just sad. Tim, who I'd met in band, made me laugh despite it all.

Now it was my turn for a long pause. I looked at Maurice. What would Dog do?

"Jessica, you there?" he asked, loudly. "Sorry, we're out at Green Mill. It's a zoo."

I pictured the scene I'd always imagined: him and me, out together with a group of friends at Green Mill or some other restaurant, at a table in the center of the room. But it wasn't to be.

"That's okay. No . . . it's not much better." I began cataloging my Rondo mistakes over the phone. I ended up telling him about Mr. Aaron's manga club offer. "What do you think I should do?"

"It sounds like the perfect thing. You should go for it. Trust your heart." I agreed, and we hung up. But I thought he shouldn't be saying anything about my heart, since he'd broken it.

9

A LOUD THUD THAT SEEMED TO ECHO

"Who is that?" I heard some girl whisper when I entered the room.

Timing was everything. Never be late to class, since that meant having to walk by every set of staring eyes. But being first to class was just as bad. It allowed each person to look you over as they came in the door. Actually, first was worse, because as each person came in, they saw you alone. And people rarely came in alone, so groups of people saw you by yourself. I thought

I'd shown up in eleventh-grade science right on time. Wrong again.

Most people were in their groups, but a couple people sat alone, earbuds in, eyes down. Some looked asleep, while others were rowdy. I'd seen all these juniors around school, but I only cared about one. And Juan wasn't here yet.

"Hey, new girl, what's your name?" a girl with dark skin yelled across the room.

"Jessica."

For some reason, this drew giggles from the girl and her friends. Most of them, like the speaker, rocked the hood look hard.

"What kind of name is that for a sister?" the same girl asked. My name and light skin sometimes confused white people, but black people saw my hair and they knew. I just turned up my music, looked for an open seat, and willed the clock to move faster.

"Hey, Miss Mulatto, I'm talking to you!"

I stopped. Even louder music couldn't drown out how offensive that word was. I turned and started to leave.

"Jasmine, back off," I heard some girl say from behind me.

"Wanna make me?" the loud girl, Jasmine, countered.

Then the two girls stared at each other like each was daring the other to fight.

"Have a seat," came an adult voice—Mr. Hunter, the teacher. Everybody scampered back to their chairs. I'd been distracted and hadn't planned an escape route.

"Sit with us," said a cute, curvy Latina girl. There were several empty seats around the room.

"We got a spot," came another voice, a girl from the back of the room.

I was all deer-in-headlights, standing in the middle of the room with every eye on my blushing face, my sweating pits, my metal-mouth, and my hideous clothes.

"Miss Johnson, have a seat, please," Mr. Hunter said, and I froze.

He repeated his request, not quite as nicely. The room started buzzing like an angry beehive.

"Over here," someone shouted to laugher. Then every class clown asked me to sit next to them. One guy pointed at his lap, another held up a chair and offered it to me. I stayed frozen like ice.

"As soon as Miss Johnson sits, we can start." More buzzing, some in Spanish.

The door behind me opened. I wondered if it would be the principal and the people from the crazy house coming for me.

"Sorry I'm late," a young male voice said. I stopped staring at the floor. It was Juan, from the store. "I had a busy morning with—"

"Juan, see me after class," Mr. Hunter said, but not in a scolding way.

Juan walked past me to a table on the left side of the room, far from the door. He sat next to the curvy Latina and whispered something to her. On the other side of him was an empty chair.

But only for a moment. "Hey, girl from the store," Juan said as he waved for me to sit next to him. I tried to hide my face as walked over, my cheeks burning. "This is my cuz, Selena."

"Jessica Johnson." I dropped my heavy camo book bag on the floor next to me. It landed with a loud thud that seemed to echo through the room of new faces, new judges, and one Juan Fernandez.

10

MAYBE NOT SO CRAZY AFTER ALL

"I can't prescribe medications, Jessica, but I can certainly recommend a psychiatrist who can," Nina Martin said. That was my first question to start off our session together. "Or perhaps your family doctor could consult with me to consider prescribing something."

"I want 'em all: antidepressants, antianxiety, beta-blockers, whatever else will help."

The psychologist laughed. "You know, I sometimes long for the old days, before the

Internet, when patients didn't think they knew more about their treatment than health professionals do."

I slumped in my chair. "Everything else seems so hard," I confessed. I saw enough kids with pills at Rondo. Drugs seemed like an easy out.

"Cognitive behavior therapy *is* hard work, and that is why it's effective," she explained. Her suit today was light brown, and her mood was once again chipper; she was a chipmunk.

"The diagnosis instrument we worked on last time has helped identify areas that we—"

"You're throwing me into the deep end of the pool, aren't you?" I asked. "You're going to make me speak in class?"

Dr. Martin gave another smile. "Well, you're correct that part of the process will involve exposure therapy, in which we'll confront fears such as public speaking by facing them."

No smile from me. "What's all this *we* stuff? I'm the one you're making do everything."

"That's true," she said with kind of a shrug, "but remember that I can't 'make you' do anything. This is on you."

I folded my arms across my chest, hiding the ugly blue top I'd chosen. She scribbled something in her notes. Was she the fashion police, as well as Jessica's Crazy Doctor?

"I don't believe in the deep end of the pool approach," she continued. "As a matter of fact, we should begin with those items that cause the least anxiety and avoidance." She ran down the list.

I stopped her at "presenting in front of a small group" and told her about the manga club that Mr. Aaron had asked me to join.

"That is a smart choice," she said in an approving tone. "It's people your age with a common interest. And there would be no academic pressure, like there is in your classes, so it sounds like a good environment to practice in."

"That's what I thought." But I'd thought the same about softball in seventh grade, Spanish club in eighth, and band in ninth. They all seemed like good ideas until the dragon inside me caused me to flee.

"Another part of our time together will be social skill building," Dr. Martin said. "We'll role-play social situations, so again, that will be good practice for when you encounter them in the real world."

"That sounds silly." Role-play days would equal school sick days for Jessica Johnson, I decided.

"Well, then, you'll probably think the next idea is sillier. What do you know about yoga?" she asked.

"Not much."

"Look, in addition to changing thought patterns, we need to look at ways to reduce the physical symptoms of stress in your life, and yoga is one way to do that. Would you consider it?"

I nodded an okay. I knew it was a healthier stress release than smoking. And cheaper, since Skylar had stopped selling cigs.

"And finally, at the base of all of this is cognitive restructuring," she explained. "In other words, we want to change the way you think about things. Your anxiety all starts because of negative thoughts. As a kid, did you ever play dominos?" I nodded.

"The negative thoughts are like the first domino, Jessica. They set everything in motion.

We'll work to change how those pieces fall—eventually giving you a different way of thinking. That should cause your anxiety to decrease."

I looked for the tissues. She set them on the small round table next to me. "Thanks."

"Don't thank me yet, Jessica. You're going to do all the heavy lifting, and then—"

"Then I'll be normal?"

"Then you'll be Jessica, the person you were meant to be."

I didn't know whether to laugh or cry, so I did both at the same time. Jessica Johnson, maybe not so crazy after all.

11

CAN SHAMAN WARRIOR SLAY THE DRAGON?

Dylan devoured his sandwich in about four quick bites. Tonisha drank milk and dipped her hands into a box of animal crackers, eating them one at a time. Instead of my normal lunch of smoke and solitude, I sucked down Altoids with my mom's paranoid voice running through my head, telling me not to choke on them.

"So, do we want to start by telling a little about ourselves?" Mr. Aaron asked, which was odd since I knew Tonisha and Dylan from language arts. The four of us sat in Mrs. Howard-Hernandez's classroom. She ate lunch at her desk, headphones on, grading papers. "Or jump right in with manga?"

"Manga!" Dylan and Tonisha said at the same time, which made everybody laugh. Once we settled, Tonisha started talking in detail about some of her favorite series. Every now and then, Dylan would agree with something she said, or Mr. Aaron—who didn't seem to know that much about it—would ask questions. I waited my turn.

"The books are way better than the anime, way better," Tonisha said about one of my favorite series. So, just as I had practiced with Nina Martin, I stuck a toe in the shallow end.

"I agree, Tonisha." Agree with someone first, use their name, and smile. Three for three.

"What's your favorite series?" Mr. Aaron asked me. A couple times before, he had glanced at me, trying to prod me with his eyes to speak, but now he'd finally called me out.

And as I had role-played in our session and then practiced until late last night, I provided a short summary of *Kimi ni Todoke:* From Me to You. "The main character is a girl named Sadako, but her classmates call her something else because she resembles a scary character in a famous horror movie. So . . . she's feared and misunderstood because of her looks. But, despite her appearance, she's a sweet and timid girl who longs to be able to make friends with everyone and be liked by everyone. It has great artwork and stories."

"Sounds cool," Dylan said. "Is there an anime series?"

"Only on DVD in Japan, but you can find it on YouTube."

"Cool. Thanks, Jessica," Dylan said. *Thank you for that smile*, I thought.

I followed up with my well-rehearsed line. "Dylan, what is your favorite manga series?"

Dylan answered quickly, "Shaman Warrior."

We waited for details from Dylan, but none followed, so Tonisha took over. "That isn't true manga, 'cause it's not Japanese. It's manhwa. Like all the best series, it's Korean."

Mr. Aaron jumped in. "Why is Korean better, Tonisha?"

"First, because I speak Korean. My mom's Korean." She kept going. For someone who hadn't wanted to read her six-word memoir in front of the class, Tonisha revealed a lot. We eventually got back to books before the bell.

"So, good first meeting, everyone," Mr. Aaron said, and applauded, per usual for meetings with him.

"When do we meet next?" Dylan asked Mr. Aaron.

"How about once a week, on Thursdays at lunch?" Heads nodded all around, including mine.

Tonisha started to talk about the anime club at her old high school while I gathered up my things. I popped in another Altoid and started toward the door. "Jessica, wait up."

I turned. Dylan stood behind me. He was all gangly arms and legs, and that goofy smile.

"Oh, before the next meeting, I'd like you all to do something," Mr. Aaron called out.

"What's that?" Tonisha asked, tossing her empty box of crackers in the trash.

"Go out and recruit more members," Mr.

Aaron said. "Talk to all your friends."

The smile that had been on my face quickly vanished.

"Yeah, right," Dylan said. "I don't think we need any more people, do you, Jessica?" Dylan asked.

I could feel my blushing face turning redder than red, so I quickly shook my head no. I wondered if there was any chance Dylan the Shaman Warrior could slay the dragon inside.

12

THE NEXT LEVEL

Dad and I sat in the therapist's waiting room. Mom was not feeling well and was in the bathroom down the hall. (We knew it was bad if she was using a public toilet—"so many germs.") Suddenly Dad broke the silence.

"I'm proud of you," he said.

"Really?"

"Yes."

"Thanks." Like most conversations with Dad, it wasn't so much a dialogue as a single word from each of us.

"For what?" I asked. He just pointed at the door to Nina Martin's office.

"It's hard," I confessed. "Like trying to get to the next level of a video game."

"Yeah? Is it a little fun too?" Not only did I get more two words, I managed to get Dad's attention away from his phone. He didn't make much eye contact, but the focus was on me.

With just the two of us in the waiting room, and him for once not sucked into cyberspace, I told Dad about therapy. It seemed the meds Dr. Lane had prescribed—an antidepressant and an antianxiety—had kicked in, at least a little.

"We're both proud of you," he said.

"Thanks."

And then we returned to a normal Darryl-and-Jessica-Johnson conversation of long pauses and one-word sentences, distracted by our devices.

They'd said before that they were proud of me, but usually it was Mom, and it was always for the stuff that came easy, like schoolwork. They'd never said a word for or against when I joined and then dropped various groups, going all the way back to an ill-fated Girl Scout experience. Were the meds and therapy sessions the cheat code I needed to reach the next level?

○ ○ ○

As always, I started the session reviewing the twos and threes from my test.

Nina Martin looked at me for a second, like she was sizing me up. "Now that you're working on the treatment plan and you're on some meds to stabilize things, I think it's time to push yourself. You can choose which, but let's tackle one of these threes."

"Why not another two?"

"Well, like you said about moving science classes, it seems you respond best to challenge." I of course hadn't told her the real reason I jumped to eleventh-grade science—Juan—so it was time.

She nodded, scribbled, smiled, and nodded more. "That's real progress."

"I didn't mean to lie to you," I confessed. "I was embarrassed, that's all."

"Well, you're taking on a lot right now, Jessica," she said. "So I don't expect everything to be perfect. Therapy, like life, is untidy."

I thought about our house—that's what it felt like sometimes, that Dad and I were messy boarders in Mom's perfectly kept house. "Maybe I'll try talking in a group or something."

"Jessica, you choose, but remember what we talked about last time." She leaned closer and put her hand on the edge of my chair. "Control your breathing, which will relax you. Think about, write down, or even rehearse what you want to say. Ask yourself the reality-check questions we talked about. But most importantly, don't let fear take away your power."

"I know."

"Social anxiety disorder isn't your fault, but it is in your power to overcome it."

"I know."

"Relax, Jessica. You're getting there."

13

DEEPEST BREATH, THEN INTO THE DEEP END

I dropped the heavy bag from my late afternoon library score onto my bedroom floor. In addition to my usual manga stash, I'd picked up another book on social anxiety disorder, a yoga DVD, and some books from Dylan's favorite series, Shaman Warrior.

Mom began her tedious process of unpacking the items we got at the store on the way back from the library. Dad offered me a soda and then took his sixty-four ounces of Dew downstairs.

See you tomorrow.

"I'm taking the dog for a walk," I yelled toward the kitchen and basement. The *W* word and sound of the leash brought Maurice to the front door, tail wagging in anticipation. Like me each morning before science class, sort of. Mr. Hunter pushed small-group work in his eleventh-grade class, since it was more lab focused. Selena was my lab partner, and Juan was my tablemate. Like with Tim back at Verdant Hill, the closeness brought conflicting feelings of crush and being crushed.

When I arrived at the swings, I pulled out the last cigarette from the pack. I savored it as I looked at my phone and admired the growing list of contacts: Tonisha, Dylan, Selena, Skylar, and Juan. Add me, and my six-word Rondo memoir could be a list of names.

After I finished the cigarette, trying to swing through the smoke rings I'd blown, I visited Juan's Facebook page. When he'd asked about my page, I told him half of the truth: that my mom didn't want me to have one. With her fears about online predators and perverts, that wasn't a lie. But the whole truth was sadder. Other than Tim and a couple of his friends from band, I had no online friends. And even Tim and his friends hardly ever posted. I went crazy at first, posting links and even some of my manga drawings, but nothing. No comments. My online life was a ghost town. The only thing missing was tumbleweeds.

Juan, Selena, and Tonisha had hundreds of friends and plenty of action on their pages. Only Dylan didn't seem to be online. Only Dylan didn't have many friends at school, other than Tonisha and me. I started to call his number but hung up before it started ringing.

Behind me in the park, I heard the noises of a late fall afternoon. There were children playing and sounds of family get-togethers. As I stared at Dylan's number, I wondered what my life would be like if things were different in my family. If Mom's family hadn't more or less disowned her for marrying Dad, if my parents weren't as messed up, if I had brothers or sisters, even nieces and nephews, then would something as easy as dialing a phone number not be quite so hard? I kept imagining it as I pushed the Call button again.

"Hi, Dylan? It's Jessica." I petted Maurice as I spoke, and it helped calm me a little.

"Oh, hi," Dylan said softly. "What's going on?"

I could almost see the words I'd practiced, scrolling like on a movie marquee in front of me. The therapist had said I could write down what I wanted to say, but I shouldn't use the paper on the actual call. I controlled my breathing like she'd taught me. "I picked up a Shaman Warrior."

"Good call." Did he mean it was good I called? Why did I overanalyze everything?

"But, the library just had volumes five and six."

"I own them all," he said. "I could loan—"

"Or maybe you could . . ." I petted Maurice's head so hard I probably gave him a concussion.

"Or maybe?"

Deepest breath, then into the deep end. "Maybe at lunch you could tell me what happens?"

14

SIT. STAY. ROLL OVER. GOOD DOG.

"Is Skylar here yet?" I asked Juan before school. I had money in my pocket ready to burn on smokes. "I heard he was selling again."

Juan laughed. I hoped it wasn't at me. "Don't be saying stuff like that out loud."

"As if I'd talk too much."

More laughter—with me, not at me, it seemed. Although the joke was on me in science. I'd joined the eleventh-grade class mostly to be around Juan, but when we got assigned lab partners for a big final project, he wasn't in my group. In my group were three strangers, which meant tackling another two on my list of stressors.

"Sorry, I didn't know," I replied.

"I'll let him know you're looking for him," Juan said and offered me a fist bump. The thin skin of my hand pressed for a microsecond against his tough-as-nails knuckles.

"Hey, did you hear about this party coming up?" Selena asked. I turned to leave.

"Jessica, you gotta hear this," Selena said, and she was off and running about some party. She touched my arm, as if to pull me back into the group. Their group. My group? "So what do you think?"

What did I think about a party where everyone was going, except no one had invited me? "Sounds like fun," I lied. I barely knew the kid hosting it, and while maybe Selena and Juan were my group, neither had actually invited me to the party. I couldn't believe I'd fooled myself with Juan—as if someone that cool and connected would like me.

I bummed a smoke off Juan, let the techno from my headphones invade my ears, and walked, head down, back behind the school, away from the other smokers, to my fortress of solitude.

◦ ◦ ◦

I wasn't called on in any of my morning classes, so I arrived in language arts unscathed but still nursing my wounds from the conversation before school. On my way to my assigned spot, I stopped by Dylan's seat. As on most days, he was drawing fantastic manga characters. I wondered if I'd fooled myself with Dylan too.

"Dylan, on for the lunch?" I tapped his shoulder. He nodded but never looked up. Eye contact wasn't his strongest suit, but I also wasn't eye candy like some of the girls here.

"Jessica, a moment please," Mrs. Howard-Hernandez said, way too loud. Other students might have generated the you're-in-trouble-now buzz, but my drama earned only indifference.

She motioned for me to sit, and like a good dog, I obeyed. "The end of the marking period is coming up, and you still have an incomplete from the first assignment."

"Maybe I'll take the F."

"Why would you want to do that? You've done well on other assignments," she asked. "Lots of people are afraid of public speaking. It's a big fear, but I think I can help you, if you give me a chance."

"It's more than that, and you know it," I hissed.

"No, I don't." The second bell rang. "Stay after, and we'll talk."

"Today?"

"Today." The tone wasn't a request, it was an order. Sit. Stay. Roll over. Good dog.

✿ ✿ ✿

I told Mrs. Howard-Hernandez about my disorder. She was sympathetic, but the incomplete stood. Still, telling her was a step forward. The lack of a party invite from Juan had felt like a step back, so the outcome of the day hinged on Dylan. All I needed was something normal, a nice boy-girl conversation that maybe led to flirting and then, maybe, who knew.

"Dylan, I'm sorry I'm late—" That was as far I got into my speech and into the old home economics classroom where he'd asked to meet. There stood Dylan, my partner in this nice, normal conversation, wearing a black dress. One step forward, one step back, and one kick in the guts.

15

TWO WORDS AND ANOTHER BIG LEAP

The dress was actually a cloak worn by a character in Shaman Warrior, Dylan explained at manga club.

Dylan handed out flyers to me, Tonisha, and three new members Tonisha had brought. The flyers were for an upcoming cosplay event at the St. Paul Convention Center.

"Cosplay? What the freak is that?" one of the new girls asked. Like Tonisha, she was dark-skinned, but she was thin like me. Big glasses, short hair, Chucks, and an attitude I liked.

"*Cosplay* is short for costume play, where people wear costumes based on characters from fiction, like manga and anime," Dylan said, way too fast. Whenever he was called on to answer questions in class, he talked so fast he was hard to understand. I didn't know if it was a speech thing, or maybe he didn't like to talk in class, so when he had to, it was like he wanted to pull off the Band-Aid quickly. "I'm making a new Shaman Warrior costume."

"You make your own costumes?" Tonisha asked. "Like sewing and stuff?"

Dylan nodded.

"I don't know how to sew," Tonisha said. The three newbies said they didn't either.

I waited for Dylan to offer to teach them, but he said nothing. I didn't know much about it. Mom never taught me some of that basic stuff other people seemed to know. I'd just done some sewing on my own. I'd heard about the convention but never dreamed of going.

"I know a little about sewing," I said toward

the floor. "Maybe Dylan and I could teach everyone."

"I don't know about playing dress-up," said the new girl with attitude.

"Shatika, you don't know nothin' about nothin'," Tonisha said, and laughed. "You stick with Tonisha, and I'll teach you some things you need to know."

Shatika laughed too. "Alright," she answered. Mr. Aaron then asked her and the two other girls to introduce themselves to the group. All three were eleventh-graders that Tonisha knew from Central High School. They didn't talk about why they were at Rondo—nobody usually did. If you were here, it was for a good reason, but nobody's business.

"Any luck recruiting anyone else, Dylan? Jessica?" Mr. Aaron asked. "That's okay, we got enough right now. Who wants to start the conversation today?"

He hardly needed to ask since Tonisha always went first. She was funny, which everybody liked, and profane, which Mr. Aaron called her out on, but she was always the center of attention. *I don't need to be like her,* I thought, *but I need people like her to like me.*

Dylan and I did get a chance to talk again, mainly because Mr. Aaron steered the conversation our way. I said a few words about Shaman Warrior, but Dylan didn't react. When I spoke, he seemed to concentrate more on his drawing than on my words.

As the bell rang, Mr. Aaron said, "Good meeting! Same time next week?"

"Can we talk more about the convention next time?" Dylan asked quietly.

Mr. Aaron agreed as he joined the rest of us walking to the door to get to class.

"Jessica, can I ask you something?" Dylan asked in the same small voice.

I stopped in my tracks. I couldn't imagine what he wanted. I turned, and he motioned for me to sit across from him. I dumped my heavy bag between us as a barrier.

"Why did you act weird when you saw my costume?" His pencil pressed hard on the paper.

"It was just odd."

He laughed. "Like either one of us would

know anything about being odd, right?"

"Not at all."

He laughed. "So what was the real reason?" he asked. I owed Dylan an honest answer, like the one Tim never gave me in his let's-just-be-friends speech. Dylan added, "You know, it doesn't make me gay."

"I know," I said. Two words and then another big leap: "So can we go to the convention together?"

16

ALL CONNECTED BY A STURDY BARRIER

As always, Nina Martin had placed the yellow
box of tissues on the table, but for the first time,
I hadn't needed to reach for it. Yet.

"Jessica, I'm really pleased at the progress
you're making."

I'd noticed how when I started therapy,
everything was "we," but whenever I suc-
ceeded—which was a lot, in the time we'd been
working together—then it was all about me. She
took the blame, but never the credit. "I wish I

would've done this sooner," I said.

"Don't bother with regrets, Jessica," she said. "Focus on the positive."

"It's just that, what if in junior high, when I first noticed how stressed out I got at small things that seemed so easy for everybody else, what if I'd found you then?"

Dr. Martin set down the pad and pen that took notes on my life. "'What if' doesn't help."

I nodded in agreement. *What if* were the two most dangerous words in the dictionary.

"And Jessica, you probably were not ready, not mature enough yet to work through a treatment plan."

Another nod from me; it was definitely work. But like Dad said, that's what made something fun. Asking Dylan to go the convention put me up one more level. I was gaining powers.

"Jessica, like any journey, there might be setbacks, but you're getting more resilient." She picked up the pad and paper again. "One of the hardest things is managing expectations."

"If I don't have any, then I won't be disappointed," I joked. She didn't even smile.

"One key to cognitive restructuring is set-ting realistic goals and developing realistic expectations," she said. "We're trying to get you in a balanced place. A safe, normal place."

"I don't know if I can ever be normal, living with my parents." I cataloged Mom's high anxi-ety and Dad's dulling depression. "That's what I came from."

"Like most things in our lives, Jessica, social anxiety disorder is a combination of nature and nurture. You probably have a genetic tendency, but that's it, a tendency. You have control."

"I guess I feel that now, but sometimes I'm not so sure."

The therapist pivoted in her chair and grabbed a folder from her desk. "Before you came in today, I looked over the list of the things you've accomplished because you've taken control."

She handed me the sheet of paper filled with crossed-out bullet points. Each bullet point was a reminder of who I was; each cross-off was a reminder of who I was becoming. I had spoken in groups, spoken to someone I was attracted to—actually two someones, both Dylan and Juan—and many other things that would've sent me into full-blown meltdown at the start of the year.

"But you've got a few more items on our list," she reminded me. "You still have yet to give your oral report and speak in front of your class, and you still haven't attended a party."

I told her about the big Rondo party coming up that everyone but me was going to attend. Just talking about it messed up my breathing.

"Well, maybe we're taking this too literally. Maybe it could be any social event."

"Like a convention or a gathering of people I didn't know?"

"I suppose, yes, that would have many of the same elements of being surrounded by strangers and pushing yourself to interact with them. What do you have in mind, Jessica?"

I told her about the upcoming cosplay convention. She seemed actually interested.

"Well, that would certainly be a stressful event. Do you think you're ready for it?"

I nodded and then told her more about

Dylan, which led to telling her about Tim, which led to every other thing connected by the sturdy barrier of social anxiety that I'd built up and now needed to tear down.

She scribbled and smiled as I spoke, but I didn't tell her the best part about cosplay: I could put on a costume and, for a few hours, be someone else—or really, just be free to be myself. I reached for the tissues.

17

SORRY, NOT SORRY

My science class reminded me of the bar scene in *Star Wars*: a bunch of aliens with nothing in common except for sharing a space at the same time. Our latest addition was Calvin, a new big-mouth at Rondo who reminded me of every bully at Verdant Hill. Mr. Hunter had already had harsh words to shut Calvin up so that we could hear about our next assignment.

"This is your final project, and it accounts for one-third of your grade," Mr. Hunter said. I forced myself to breathe deeply as he explained that we'd be doing group projects involving a presentation. That was two threes, working with a group and presenting to a crowd, thrown together. I wondered if Nina Martin would let me count it as a six to cross off my list.

"Each group will choose a topic," Mr. Hunter continued. "Discuss and decide on one that all four of you agree on."

I got up and started for the front of the room, where Mr. Hunter kept the bathroom key. But I didn't get far before I tripped over Calvin's out-stretched leg. I hit the floor loud—though not as loud as the laughter that followed.

"Clumsy. It must be all the words stuck in her metal mouth," Calvin said.

"Say another word, and you're done," Juan shouted from across the room.

Like me, Calvin shut his mouth. Was Juan really acting as my knight in shining armor?

"Gentlemen, that's quite enough," Mr. Hunter said. "Stop. Now."

I pulled myself up. I took a step toward the bathroom key but then turned and took two steps back toward Calvin.

"What is it, mute?" he whispered. His expression dared me, from his zit-filled forehead down to his stubbly bearded chin.

Clutching the table for support, I leaned in over him. "What?" I asked.

"I said that's enough!" Mr. Hunter yelled. But I hadn't had enough yet as I raised my voice and unleashed my inner dragon on Calvin's bully face, breathing fire and spewing insults directed at every person who'd ever made fun of me.

❀ ❀ ❀

Mom tapped her foot double-time, but Dad actually chuckled and said, "I never thought I'd see it." By *it*, he meant the day Jessica Johnson got in trouble for talking *too much*.

However, Mrs. Baker looked anything but amused. My profanity-laced tirade meant serious consequences. "As an alternative school, we allow our students some leeway to express themselves, but Jessica..." And she stopped talking, like she was too amazed at the morning's events to go on.

"I'm sorry," I whispered, even though I wasn't. Not one bit. I don't know if verbally tearing a bully apart with everyone watching counted as "speaking in front of the class," but it seemed good enough. After class, more than one person told me what I did was cool. Juan and Selena were the first to congratulate me.

"At the same time, from Mr. Hunter's report, it's clear that Jessica was provoked." Mrs. Baker rattled off the events for my parents. "So after some consideration, Jessica will get a one-day suspension."

I said nothing, out of relief. My parents nodded, understanding that it could've been much worse.

"Mr. Hunter also said that he thought Jessica was doing much better at participating in class," Mrs. Baker continued. "I've had similar reports from other teachers, and Mr. Aaron says he enjoys her contributions to the manga club. Despite this morning's events, she's been a fine addition to Rondo."

With that, Mom and Dad's expressions lifted into smiles, rare genuine smiles, and this meeting to discuss my punishment suddenly felt more like a reward.

* * *

"Jessica . . ." It seemed that Nina Martin, hiding a smile, couldn't find the right words after I told her about the events of the day. "Questionable behavior aside, it's another sign of progress. But you still need to give your oral report. Why do you think you were able to talk in front of everyone today?"

I thought about it. "I didn't feel people judging me or making fun of me, because I just didn't think about it."

"Exactly, Jessica. One of your issues is that you overthink words and actions before an interaction—"

I finished her sentence. "And then I over-analyze everything afterward. It's a bad cycle."

She nodded in agreement. "With our work here and your medications, you're making real progress, but I want to give you more tools in case you feel the dominos starting to fall again."

Turning toward her desk, she lifted a sheet of

paper. Was it my therapy report card, completed? "This is the address for the Social Anxiety Support website. It has lots of information, but more importantly, it has a forum for teens. These online groups can be a real source of support, especially from your peers. You've done well here with me, so I think you're ready."

I stuffed the paper into my purse, next to my cosplay convention ticket.

"I hope you'll follow up on that, Jessica. You can lurk; you don't even need to post."

"To be honest, I'm a little afraid," I said. "Not of what people might think, but that I'll get sucked in, and soon I'll be like my dad, living more online than in real life."

The psychologist set her pad and pen aside and leaned in, meeting my eyes. "It's about choices, Jessica."

I nodded. "I'm trying to make the right choices, but it's hard to know."

"That's what cognitive behavioral treatment is all about," she said. "It's giving you the tools to become your own healing therapist and stop being your own harshest critic."

18

I LIKE EVERYTHING ABOUT YOU, EXCEPT

I was wrong. My science class wasn't the *Star Wars* bar scene; the cosplay convention at the St. Paul Convention Center was. Except it was the bar scene on steroids. More than a thousand people in costumes filled every inch of the massive old building. It looked as if magic had brought every science fiction and fantasy action flick to life. It was bright inside but was made even brighter by the constant, blinding flashes of cameras and phones.

"Over here!" Tonisha shouted as Dylan and I made our way to our arranged meeting place. I almost hadn't made it, since Mom had all sorts of concerns, but I made a rare stand and won parental approval. Dad even agreed to drive Dylan and me. As always, Dad didn't say much in the car—not that he could have gotten a word in, since Dylan and I talked most of the way about Shaman Warrior and the convention. Yet, the entire car ride, I noticed Dad's sly little smile.

Tonisha and the other three girls were decked out as characters from the manwha Bride of the Water God. Tonisha was dressed as Soah, the lead character.

"You all look great!" Dylan said.

"You're just saying that because you made the costume!" Tonisha replied, nearly yelling to be heard over all the other noise.

"Teach a man to sew and he'll make a hundred costumes, right, Jessica?" Dylan asked.

"Who?" I asked. "Who is this Jessica of which you speak?"

"Sorry, I mean Sawako!"

I wore a long black wig with straighter hair than I'll ever have, a flowing, white multilayered dress, and my character's signature red bow tie. I wasn't Jessica. I was Sawako, the main character of From Me to You, the misunderstood girl who just wants to be liked and then finds Kazehaya, the boy she's longed for all her life. Dylan was dressed as the Shaman Warrior. Everybody could be somebody else today.

Tonisha and the girls joked back and forth. They made fun of each other's costumes, not in a mean or bully way, but how I recalled friends did such things. When they did the same to me, I didn't feel stressed. They were including me through insults. *Friendship is one crazy cracker*, I thought.

"So, what do you want to do first?" Jasmine asked.

The four girls crowded around the program, discussing all the events. There were talks, contests, celebrities, games, panels, autographs, and even a cosplay prom. I'd hoped Dylan and I could attend, but it was a nonissue since Mom wanted me home before it even began.

"You did a nice job with them," I said to Dylan, pointing at the girls' costumes. He and I had helped the four design and make their outfits. Since Mrs. Baker always stayed late to run the after-school program and detention, she'd allowed us to use the old home ec room. I doubt that room had ever been filled with as much laughter before. I know that no classroom I'd ever been in had brought me as much laughter, at least. Maybe for people like Tonisha, that came easy, but to Jessica—to Sawako—it did not. "And I had a blast helping," I added.

"I had fun, but mostly hanging with you," Dylan said. I hoped my heavily made-up face masked my blushing cheeks. "Too bad we couldn't stay for the prom. That might have been fun."

"Well according to my mom, all the people in costumes make it very dangerous," I reported.

Dylan laughed. "Maybe next year . . ."

I paused. I had thought that proms and dances were stupid, but maybe that was only because I knew I'd never go. "Maybe."

"If we could dress like this for a school prom, that would be something."

"I don't think Rondo has a prom," I said. "But if it did, I doubt it would be *that* alternative."

He smiled. "You're funny. I like that about you. To be honest, I like almost everything about you."

I was pretty sure this was him flirting, so I took the bait. "Almost?"

"Except I don't like the smell of smoke on you."

My smile turned into a pout, which gave Dylan a soft landing space for our first kiss.

19

My life aloud in six words

On the day before our term final, I had to
present my six-word memoir to the class. The
night before, I read over the paper and chose
two to read aloud. Then I did my yoga exer-
cises, did my breathing routines, rubbed Maurice's belly, and thought about cosplay, Dylan,
and everything else that brought me pleasure.
When I felt the first anxiety domino start to
tip, I jumped online to the teen forum, where
people like me all over the world were fighting

similar stress monsters. My fellow dragon slayers calmed me down so that the next morning, I was ready.

The paper had twelve memoirs, two more than required. I thought I should do more to make up the incomplete. And even though Nina Martin stressed living in the present, I knew my past—and my parents' past—was an important part of my story. I wrote one for Dad.

Please emerge from basement, engage now

And I wrote one for Mom.

Scared of dying, avoids really living

Mrs. Howard-Hernandez called roll and tried to get students settled, hard to do with everyone eager for the break. We would have the final test tomorrow and then some days off while the teachers finished grades. In all the classes where I hadn't needed to talk much, where the teachers didn't challenge me, I knew I'd earned As. But in language arts and science, I'd let my disorder take control, and my grades had suffered. All I could hope was that they'd heard the improvement.

"Before we start, Jessica needs to read her

six-word memoir," Mrs. Howard-Hernandez announced to the class.

Around the room, I sensed that people realized this was a big deal for me. As I got up in front of everyone, I asked myself six questions.

Were people really staring, rather than just looking at me? No.

Were they really judging me? No.

Were they really making fun of me? No.

Did it really matter what they thought? No.

Was I stressed out? Yes.

But could I control the stress? Yes.

It was a technique Dr. Martin had taught me, among so many others.

"Since I'm so late in doing this, I'm doing two," I said. I set the paper quickly on Mrs. Howard-Hernandez's desk. I could remember twelve words, especially since I probably couldn't stop my hands from shaking if I held up the page.

"The first is about what I'm not. Here we go." Deep breath, relax, thanks Dr. Martin. Eyes for once not on the floor, but on the sea of friendly faces. "Not shy, not sad, not silent."

Dylan applauded the loudest, although Tonisha was a close second. I imagined for a moment that Juan, Selena, and Skylar were also in the audience. Others too: Mr. Aaron became my father, Mrs. Howard-Hernandez stood in for my mother. Across the miles, Tim sat in a Verdant Hill classroom, but in my mind he was here with me now.

"So, here's my life aloud in six words," I said, clear and strong: "My new life starts right now."

AUTHOR'S NOTE

According to the Social Anxiety Support website (www.socialanxietysupport.com), Social Anxiety Disorder is defined as "a mental health diagnosis used to describe a level of social anxiety that is so distressing, excessive, and/or pervasive that it is significantly interfering with an individual's quality of life. The feared or avoided situations in social phobia can be very narrow and specific, or may extend to the majority of one's interactions with others" ("Social Anxiety Disorder and Social Phobia: Symptoms and Treatment," *Social Anxiety Support*, 2014, http://www.socialanxietysupport.com/disorder/).

I spent a great deal of time lurking on the various forums on that website, in particular the teen support page. In addition to reading various posts, I also reached out and asked for research subjects, so thanks to Amanda, Genelia, Jacob, Jenna, Kori, Manon, Martim, Nicky, Shane, and Shelia Rae for sharing their stories and answering my questionnaire.

Another helpful resource was *What You Must Think of Me: A Firsthand Account of One Teenager's Experience with Social Anxiety Disorder*, by Emily Ford (Oxford University Press, 2007).

In addition to my own research, Nancy McLean reviewed the manuscript for accuracy of my portrayal of social anxiety disorder and the therapeutic process. McLean is a Licensed Marriage and Family Therapist (LMFT) with a graduate degree and clinical work experience. Along with a two- to three-year master's program with a practicum and internship, LMFTs are required to complete clinical training in individual or family therapy.

Finally, as with all the books in The Alternative series, students and teachers at the South

Saint Paul Community Learning Center read and commented on the manuscript, in particular John Egelkrout, Mindy Haukedahl, Kathleen Johnson, and Lisa Seppelt.

ABOUT THE AUTHOR

Patrick Jones is the author of more than twenty novels for teens. He has also written two non-fiction books about combat sports: *The Main Event*, on professional wrestling, and *Ultimate Fighting*, on mixed martial arts. He has spoken to students at more than one hundred alternative schools, including residents of juvenile correctional facilities. Find him on the web at www.connectingya.com and on Twitter: @PatrickJonesYA.